our
generation®

This is Alice's story.

A very special thanks to the editor,
Joanne Burke Casey.

Our Generation® Books is a registered trademark of Maison Joseph Battat Ltd.
Text copyright © 2013 by Susan Love
ISBN: 978-0-9883165-4-6
Printed in China

For Sophie and Cindy,
idea-makers extraordinaire.

Read all the adventures in the
Our Generation® Book Series

Read more about **Our Generation®** books and dolls online:
www.ogdolls.com

CONTENTS

EXTRA! EXTRA! READ ALL ABOUT IT!
Big words, wacky words, powerful words, funny words...
what do they all mean? They are marked with this symbol *.
Look them up in the Glossary at the end of this book.

Chapter One

GRANDMA GOODIE'S NEWS

On my last report card, Mr. Zapple, my teacher, noted that I have a "very *active* imagination."

My dad says that I'm a "magnificent daydreamer."

At least once in every softball game, my coach encourages me from the third base sideline to "Stay focused, Alice!" or "Keep your head in the game, Alice!"

My book club leader mentioned to my mom that my "mind wanders," but she often wonders where it goes.

I prefer to think that I "dream big."

A perfect example is one morning in math class. Mr. Zapple began class by drawing a pizza on the whiteboard. He cut it into ten pieces, and then erased two slices.

While his lesson about subtraction continued, I started thinking about how much I love pizza. And why it's only served at the school cafeteria on the first Monday of the month. How unfair!

That gave me a grand idea: when I'm elected President of the United States, I'll pass a law that says students will be offered pizza *every* day. Free of charge. As much as you want!

In my mind I saw piping hot, super-sized, extra-gooey pizzas on all of the cafeteria tables. Happy students were gobbling them up, thrilled about the new pizza rule.

As President, I'd visit a different school each day and get to eat pizza with the kids. And while I was there, I'd give everyone the day off from doing homework.

My stomach actually began growling and I felt hungry even though lunchtime wasn't for another two hours.

"Alice," I heard Mr. Zapple say, "are you still with us on this pizza thing?"

Parker, my friend who sits next to me, turned and whispered in a joking tone, "Earth to Alice, oh Earth to Alice…"

"Pizza?" I asked, startled. "Oh yes, Mr. Zapple! I'm with you on that, all right." I glanced at the whiteboard and saw that three more slices had been erased. I realized he was actually talking about the subtraction pizza and not about my presidential plan for pizza.

11

I've had a lot of practice dreaming up stories that are fun and exciting (and sometimes tasty). But not in my wildest dreams could I have imagined that I'd jump into a real live mystery.

And I definitely would not have thought that it would all begin with a ginormous* clown shoe.

♣ ♣

Before I get to the clown shoe, a little background will help explain the scene. Every day after school I'd been helping my Grandma Goodie set up her new store, Goodie's Costume Shop, which is on the first floor of her big, old house.

We were unpacking boxes of new and donated costumes and hanging them on racks. There were creature costumes (such as lobsters, bears, hippos, beavers and sharks); character costumes (sumo wrestlers, hula dancers, ogres, witches and leprechauns); and holiday costumes

(Santa Clauses, Valentine's Day cupids and Chinese New Year dragons).

One table offered a display of hats, mustaches, wigs and wings. Another held pretend swords, magic wands and black glasses with fake noses attached.

Grandma pushed a very large, dusty box across the floor to me. SAVE was written across the side in big letters. "Alice honey, believe it or not, this has been in my attic for 38 years—" Her voice was drowned out by the jangling sound of bells that hung on the shop's front door.

"You go ahead and take a look," Grandma said over her shoulder, as she hurried off to see who'd stopped by.

Dust scattered in the air as I peeled the top flaps of the box open. That made me sneeze three times in a row (which, according to my mother, is supposed to bring good luck).

I started digging through the box. The first thing I took out was a large, lime-green vase filled with plastic daisies. I set it in the middle of a tall, round table with three legs that was filled with pointy elf ears, fangs and face paint.

I poked around in the box a little more and found two tickets to The Razzle-Dazzle Circus and a row of admission tickets. They looked like they were from a long, long time ago.

Grandma Goodie's dog, Betty, stuck her nose in the box, pulled out a bundle wrapped in faded yellow tissue paper, and then dropped it at my feet. I unwrapped the paper and found the most gorgeous outfit I'd ever seen: a vest covered in glittering red sequins, a fancy white shirt and a swingy black skirt. There was even a pair of sparkling red shoes. Wow!

As I hung the clothes on hangers, the "wheels" in my mind started turning. *Did this dazzling outfit once belong to a fashion model? A tap dancer? A celebrity*?*

I heard the click-click of Grandma Goodie's shoes behind me. She came around a rack of costumes, put her hands over her heart and beamed* with joy. "You found my ringmaster costume!"

I couldn't believe my ears. "Grandma, you were a ringmaster?! In a circus?!"

"Yes indeed!" she said, smiling with pride. "The Razzle-Dazzle Circus."

I thought that I knew *everything* about Grandma Goodie. She'd been a schoolteacher since my mother was little. She and my grandpa had been married for 36 years. They loved to travel and went to all kinds of exciting places before my grandpa died two years ago. After retiring* from teaching last year, Grandma decided to open Goodie's Costume Shop.

Learning that my grandmother was a ringmaster in a circus shocked* me!

That's Grandma, I thought, *always full of surprises!* Fun surprises. Creative surprises. Zany* surprises. I loved them all, but this was the best one yet!

Hearing Grandma's stories was one of the perks* of helping out at the store after school. *I can't wait to find out about her adventures in the circus,* I thought.

There was another special bonus about being at the shop, too. It meant that I got to spend more time with Silver Dawn, Grandma's beautiful white and silvery gray horse that lives in a barn behind the costume shop.

Silver Dawn and the other rescue animals run and play in a meadow that leads right up to the shop's back steps. Grandma adopted the animals over the past couple of years to give them better lives.

In addition to Silver Dawn and Betty, there's a friendly pig named Romeo, a white cow named Pearl, a fluffy cat named Jellybean and a bossy rooster named Toodles.

Grandma was opening the costume shop to raise money to run the farm. She's all about helping everyone—people *and* animals. I felt good about being part of that, too.

Grandma certainly makes life interesting. Little did I know that life was about to get a whole lot *more* interesting.

Chapter Two

BIG SHOES TO FILL

The ringmaster's outfit wasn't the only costume in the box. I also found a black-and-white polka-dotted clown suit with a ruffled collar and red pompom trim. There was even a matching cone-shaped hat and pair of extra, extra, extra long clown shoes.

I laughed out loud at the clown shoes. *They're HUGE!* I thought. *I wonder what it feels like to walk in these funny things.*

Unable to resist finding out, I slipped my feet inside the shoes, tied the red laces and noisily shuffled* across the floor.

The shoes felt enormous and clunky*. When I wiggled my toes, something bumpy slid between my left foot and the inside of the shoe.

I panicked*. Was it a hairy spider? A mouse? Eek!

I quickly kicked off the shoe. Out flew the bumpy thing, which was a crumpled piece of blue paper. I smoothed it out and read the strange words that were written on it:

Whistling icicles tiny helicopters many yo-yo fizzy lollipops owls whistling every rosy song

It's not a grocery list, I thought. *And it's not the kind of note you'd pass in class. So what in the world does it mean?* I thought about it for a few minutes, shrugged* and stuffed the strange message into my pocket.

Grandma hung a fuzzy, yellow duck costume on the rack next to me. It had an orange beak above the face opening and rubbery webbed feet. She spotted the polka-dotted clown outfit. "Smooch's costume!" she cried with delight.

"Who's Smooch?" I asked.

"Smooch is one of my dearest friends," Grandma said. "She used to be a clown in the circus with me way back when. Her real name is Irene."

"Why do you call her Smooch?" I wondered.

"She got that nickname in the circus and it stuck. She always blew kisses to the audience until another clown carted her off the stage in a wheelbarrow." Grandma grinned at the thought. "It was part of the show."

She fished through the box and pulled out a framed photo. "Here she is," Grandma said, pointing to a cute clown wearing the polka-dotted costume, hat and shoes.

"Who is the movie star with her arm around Smooch's shoulders?" I asked.

"Why, that's me when I was 25 years old!" exclaimed Grandma Goodie. "See? I'm wearing the ringmaster outfit that you found a few minutes ago. And look, I always put a glittery red heart on my cheek."

She looked so glamorous!

At home that night, I was sitting at my desk writing out my French homework before dinner. I reached into my pocket for an eraser and my fingertips touched the slip of paper instead. I'd forgotten all about it.

Whistling icicles? Yo-yo fizzy lollipops? Could this be a code? I wondered.

Realizing that I was daydreaming once

again, I tucked the paper back into my pocket and tried to focus on my French lesson.

It was no use. My imagination was already off and running. I knew that codes are meant to keep something secret. Maybe something valuable, like a treasure!

I dug the paper back out of my pocket and looked at the words again. I wrote "Solving the Secret Code" on the top of a sheet of notebook paper. Then I wrote down the strange words and arranged them in different ways to see if they made more sense. They didn't.

I went into the kitchen and showed my mom the slip of blue paper. "This looks like a secret code, right?" I asked. "Maybe it will lead us to a hidden treasure!"

My mom pressed her lips together to keep from smiling. She raised her eyebrows and said, "Well...I *suppose*...." The way she continued peeling potatoes made me sense that she didn't really think a treasure was likely.

Still, I couldn't help wondering.

I was still puzzling over it when I hopped onto the school bus the next morning. When I turned in my French homework that afternoon. And later on, when Grandma and I were grooming* Silver Dawn in the barn.

"The costume shop's Grand Opening Celebration is only three weeks away," Grandma said. "Let's make it really, really, really special. Any ideas?"

"I know," I said. "Since this is a costume shop, it could be a costume party!"

"Great!" Grandma praised. "Why don't we suggest a theme* for what people could dress up as?"

"Rock star costumes!" I exclaimed, hoping to dress up as my favorite singer, Gigi. I could tell that Grandma Goodie thought that theme was so-so*.

We came up with a lot more ideas: famous people from history, fairy tales, pirates, 1970s styles and book characters. Nothing seemed just right. We decided to keep brainstorming*

about it.

"Speaking of brainstorming," I said, "What do you think about this slip of paper I found in Smooch's clown shoe?" I scooped it out of my pocket. "I think it's a secret code that will lead us to a treasure."

Grandma Goodie gasped. "You're right about that!"

I was right?

"Alice honey, that *is* a code *and* it's been lost for nearly 40 years!" Grandma said.

She explained that way back when, when she'd been part of The Razzle-Dazzle Circus, she and Smooch had gone shopping one day and found a tiny top hat.

They both loved it, but there was only one. They decided to share it. Grandma wore it for one circus performance and Smooch wore it for the next performance.

For fun, when one of them was done wearing it, she'd hide it and write a secret code for the other person to figure out where the top

26

hat was hidden. This went on and on, back and forth, for a few months.

One day, Grandma lost the secret code before she figured it out. Smooch couldn't remember where she'd hidden the hat.

They searched high and low for the top hat for weeks. It was nowhere to be found. It had been a joke between Grandma and Smooch for years.

Wouldn't it be fantastic if I solved the code and found the tiny top hat? I thought to myself. *Then Grandma could wear it to the Grand Opening Celebration!*

That afternoon on my way home, my mom and I stopped by the library to check out some books about cracking* codes.

The more I read, the more fascinated I was with codes and ciphers. In a code, each *word* in a message is replaced by another *word*. In a cipher, each *letter* is replaced by another

27

letter or a *symbol**.

I also learned that throughout history, codes and ciphers have been used by scientists, spies, kings and even by an American President, Thomas Jefferson.

Some codes and ciphers have interesting or odd names, like the Saint-Cyr Slide, the Morse code and the Pigpen Cipher. It was easy to see why Grandma and Smooch had so much fun writing secret messages to each other.

My French teacher handed my homework back to me the next day at school. On the top, she'd written, "Not sure what these strange sentences mean. Please see me after class."

I could not imagine what she was talking about, until, that is, I saw my "homework."

When I'd turned in my homework, I had been daydreaming about finding a treasure. That explained why I turned in the paper from my notebook that said "Solving the Secret

Code" instead of the one that said "Alice's French Homework."

Uh-oh-pistachio!

I agreed with my teacher—I wasn't sure what the strange words meant either.

"Alice," my French teacher said gently, "how can you learn if you have your *tête dans la lune*?"

She was right again. I did have my head in the clouds. I promised her I'd try harder to concentrate in class. And I promised myself that I'd leave code-cracking *at home*.

Chapter Three

SUNRISE SURPRISE

As I said, I love surprises. Even when Grandma springs one on me at 4:30 in the morning, like she did the following Saturday. I'd slept overnight at her house after our "movie night."

"Alice honey," Grandma whispered in my ear to wake me up, "I have a surprise."

It was still dark outside when Grandma, Betty and I drove to the beach. We covered up with a cozy blanket while Betty splashed in the waves.

I was curious. What could the surprise be?

Pretty soon a brilliant sun began to peek above the ocean. It colored the sky bright orange and pink and purplish blue.

"A sunrise surprise!" I said as I gave her a long hug.

"Thanks to Smooch, this is my favorite time of the day," Grandma told me. "I knew you'd like it, too."

I was about to ask her about that, but Betty came leaping over to us, kicking sand in every direction. She wagged her tail wildly and dropped a piece of driftwood* at our feet.

After we played fetch with Betty, we went back to the barn to feed Silver Dawn and all the animals. They know the sound of Grandma's truck and always run up to the fence together to greet us when we pull into the driveway. Toodles crows and Romeo puts his snout up in the air and waves it around. It melts my heart every time.

When all were fed and given lots of TLC*, Grandma and I went into the costume shop to unpack boxes. Many people had donated their costumes to help the good cause*. While we put clothing on hangers, Grandma and I talked about everything under the sun*.

I asked Grandma tons of questions about being a ringmaster and her life in the circus. She has so many wonderful stories. Grandma told me all about my mom when she was little, and how they used to go sledding on the hill behind the farm just like I do with my mom and dad.

Grandma also showed me something special about the vase that I'd unpacked a few days earlier. The daisies are "trick" flowers that spray water out of the centers. Smooch and the other clowns used to put them on the circus stage at the beginning of each show and squirt each other—and the audience—as part of their act.

She wanted to know all about what was happening in my life, too. I acted out the home run I made in softball that won the game for our team and explained the science project that I did with my friend Maria (that sort of exploded on the way to school). I also told her every detail about my mega superstar idol*, Gigi, who is the best singer in the world.

"And guess what?" I said. "Gigi is making a special appearance at our mall the night before the shop's Grand Opening Celebration! Can you believe that?"

"If we can get this place all done before then," Grandma said, "we'll go see your rock star!"

I was thrilled. But I didn't want to get my hopes up too high. Boxes were stacked up to the ceiling, and more were arriving daily. *How*

can we possibly get them all unpacked in time? I wondered.

If there was a way to get it done, I knew Grandma would try to find it. She went out of her way to make me happy.

I wanted to make her happy, too. If only I could figure out that code and find the tiny top hat!

Grandma had given me an envelope she'd saved, filled with a whole bunch of codes and ciphers that Smooch had created for her. I'd studied them, hoping to improve my skills at cracking the code.

One was pig Latin.
It means "In your bunny slippers!"

INYAY OURYAY UNNYBAY IPPERSSLAY

Another was in Morse code for
"Under your Pillow"

••-/-•/-••/•/•-•   -•--/---/••-/•-•
•--•/••/•-••/•-••/ ---/•--

And this Backwards Cipher, which says
"in the fridge under the jelly"

yllej eht rednu egdirf eht ni

(Check out the back of the book to see
how these codes and ciphers work.)

Imagining that I was an international spy,
I got down to business and figured out all of
the secret messages, except the most important
one—Smooch's last code. I wasn't having any
luck.

It's time to call in some help, I thought.
But whom?

I snapped my fingers. Suddenly I knew
the right people for the job—the triplets—
Parker, Peyton and Phoebe. We've been friends

since we were little kids. We live in the same neighborhood and are all in the same class at school.

That afternoon, Betty came home with me. She comes over to my house on the weekends while Grandma goes to her book club.

I wrote a secret message on a piece of green paper.

Betty and I took it to the gazebo* in the park in front of my house, put a blue ballpoint pen beside it, and a rock on top of it so it wouldn't blow away.

The triplets almost always brought a picnic lunch to the gazebo on Saturday afternoons. I wanted to see if they could solve the code without my help. If they could solve this code, then it was likely they could also help me solve the circus code.

Fdq brx vroyh wklv flskhu?
Phhw ph khuh dw 3:00 s.p. wrgdb

This super-simple-to-use cipher was invented by the Roman emperor Julius Caesar. Here's how it works: each letter of the alphabet is switched with a letter that is three letters forward in the alphabet, so A is D, B is E, C is F, etc. (Look below and try it for yourself.)

a b c d e f g h i j k l m n o p q r s t u v w x y z
code = d e f g h i j k l m n o p q r s t u v w x y z a b c

37

(Try to figure it out! Did you guess? It says: "Can you solve this cipher? Meet me here at 3:00 p.m. today.")

≥ ≤

I decided to eat my PB&J sandwich on my front porch steps so I could watch for the triplets. Betty was on high alert for "her friends" (neighborhood dogs) as well as creatures of "special interest" (squirrels and rabbits).

We saw a lot of action. First I saw a woman singing and pushing a stroller through the park. Two little feet were sticking out of the stroller. A pair of squirrels chased each other up and around a tree (which made Betty's day!). And then two dads passed by with their kids who were dressed in soccer uniforms. A man with a cane crossed the park, as well as three kids doing wheelies and other tricks on their bikes. But no triplets.

A minute later, a boy who looked to be about my age came zipping through the park on a skateboard. He jumped off the skateboard, made it flip into the air, and then caught it with one hand. Pretty impressive.

I stopped in mid-chew when he entered the gazebo. What was he doing in there? It was hard to tell, but as he came out he was stuffing something into his pocket. The cipher! He must have swiped my cipher!

Chapter Four

THE CODE CREW

The triplets would be on their way to the gazebo with their picnic lunch any minute. There was no time to waste. I wrote the same secret message on another piece of green paper and grabbed Betty's leash.

Running up the gazebo steps two at a time, I stopped suddenly when I saw the first green piece of paper was *still* under the rock. However, my blue ballpoint pen was gone.

I was even more surprised when I noticed that a reply was scribbled on the bottom of the paper in the *same* code.

> Fdq brx vroyh wklv flskhu?
> Phhw ph khuh dw 3:oo s.p. wrgdb.
> RN. L'oo eh khuh dw 3:00 s.p.

I saw the front door of the triplets' house open. Quickly, I snatched the original message with the boy's writing on it and replaced it with the second message I'd just written. I put the rock on top of it and Betty and I skedaddled* across the park to my house.

Once we were back on my front porch, it took me a minute to figure out that the boy's answer was: "OK. I'll be here at 3:00 p.m."

I was thrilled. But wait, who was this kid? How did he solve the code so quickly? I puzzled it over. All I knew about him was that he was a pen thief and a pretty talented skateboarder. *And* lucky for me, he was also a crackerjack* code breaker.

❧ ❧

At five minutes to 3:00 p.m., Betty and I headed back over to the gazebo. Right away I noticed that the rock had been moved to the steps. My message was gone, which seemed like a good sign.

I had brought the envelope filled with Grandma's and Smooch's codes. Grandma had said that it was A-OK to show the other kids.

I felt nervous. What if the triplets hadn't figured out the message? They wouldn't know where to come or when.

In that case, it would be just me and the skateboarder. That could be awkward*. But as the old saying goes, two heads are better than one.

I glanced* around again. Phew! Phoebe, Peyton and Parker were headed across the park toward me. Two kids on skateboards zoomed right past them to the gazebo. It was the boy I didn't know and another kid who looked very much like him. Same height. Same smile. Even matching clothes!

Everyone had shown up, plus one more. The chances of solving the circus secret code were improving by the minute. My hopes soared.

The boy, whose name I soon found out is Alex, had moved into a house around the corner with his twin, Gracian, and their mom a few days earlier. Alex said that at his old school he had done a history project on codes and ciphers. That's how he'd recognized Julius Caesar's cipher right away.

"Sorry, I took your pen by mistake," Alex said, handing the pen back to me.

"What's this meeting all about?" Peyton asked.

"Good question," I said. "I need your help cracking a code."

That got their attention. We all sat down in the gazebo and I explained about The Razzle-Dazzle Circus, the secret code and the tiny top hat. I passed around the picture of Grandma Goodie and Smooch, as well as a few of their secret messages. The triplets and twins were fascinated by the story.

By then, it was almost dinnertime. We decided to meet again the next day at the same time.

"Sweet!" exclaimed Alex. "Let's call ourselves The Secret Code Club."

"Awesome!" said Gracian, giving Alex a high five.

"I'm in!" shouted Peyton.

"Me, too!" cried Parker.

"Me, three!" said Phoebe. She was petting Betty, who was stretched out on her side and wearing an expression of complete happiness.

I could see by the look on everyone's face

that they were all really excited.

The Secret Code Club will have the message figured out in no time, I thought. *By this time tomorrow, I'll have Grandma's top hat wrapped up and tied with a bow.*

When The Secret Code Club showed up at the gazebo the next day, they did anything *but* help solve the secret code.

I kept trying to get my friends interested in the code while they sort of half listened and fooled around.

All Phoebe wanted to do was dress Betty up in cute doll clothes she brought (including a tutu, a fancy hat, sunglasses and a sweater). Peyton was teaching herself to juggle with three tangerines. Parker was trying to set a hula-hooping record. Gracian pumped up balloons and Alex twisted them into balloon animals. He made a dog that looked like an orange version of Betty. And then Gracian made a balloon crown and stuck it on my head.

I sat fuming* on the grass—by myself—trying to solve the code. How frustrating!

It was obvious that the other kids were more interested in the idea of *performing* circus tricks than the idea of *solving* the circus clue.

Chapter Five

THINKING OUTSIDE THE BOX

Every day at Goodie's Costume Shop was like Christmas. There were boxes, boxes and more boxes to be opened. Each held surprises. I never knew what costumes I'd find. My imagination ran wild!

Was this glittering ball gown once worn by a real princess? I wondered as I lifted a long yellow-and-orange ruffled dress from a box. It was decorated with gems that sparkled like diamonds. I imagined the princess dancing in the dress as she whirled round and round the ballroom with her prince.

Was this scary mask a real bank robber's disguise? A polka-dotted dinosaur costume worn by the star in a play? An eye patch and bandana the belongings of a pirate who sailed

47

the seas long ago?

I entertained* Grandma Goodie by creating all kinds of silly stories for the costumes as we unpacked them. One of the tales I came up with made Grandma laugh so hard she had tears trickling down her face.

"You're a hoot!" she said when she caught her breath. "You have the best imagination."

That made me smile from the inside out.

Once in a while, Silver Dawn would trot up from the clover field and poke her head through the open window in the costume shop. I think she wondered what was so funny. Or maybe she was looking for a treat, which she knew was in my lunch bag.

Whenever I packed my lunch, I always added a sweet carrot to bring to Silver Dawn after school.

⸗ ⸗

A few days later, I was headed out to my school bus after the bell rang. There was Grandma Goodie, waving her arm back and forth over her head to get my attention.

"Alice honey, I have a surprise," she said, with a twinkle in her eyes. "We're taking a break from the costume business today."

She drove to a trail where we hiked up to the peak of a hill. We sat on a giant rock at the tippy top. Grandma unzipped her red backpack and handed me a square box tied with white string. Inside was a teeny-tiny, two-layer chocolate cake she'd decorated with colorful sprinkles. "Happy 9½!" was written itty-bitty in yellow icing.

"A birthday surprise!" I said, as I gave her a great big hug.

"You're exactly nine-and-a-half years old today," she said, "and that's reason to celebrate." She sang the birthday song while I cut the cake into bite-sized slices.

Grandma always jokes that she comes up with these surprises so she can get more of my hugs. I know the real reason: she likes being with me. And the feeling is mutual*.

✦ ✦

The next day was Saturday, and Phoebe, Parker, Peyton, Alex, Gracian and I met at the gazebo to crack the code. Or so I hoped.

The triplets brought their dad's unicycle* and everyone took turns practicing. Phoebe again dressed Betty up in doll clothes. Betty

loved all the attention. The other kids juggled, hula-hooped and made more balloon animals.

"C'mon guys," I pleaded. "Please let's get going and solve this clue."

"OK Alice," Peyton called, "but check this out! I can juggle four tangerines at a time now!"

"That's great, but uh…" I grumbled.

"Look, look, look!" Parker shouted. "It's my record! Six hula-hoops going at once!"

The triplets and the twins kept right on goofing around instead of getting serious. That made me *seriously* annoyed.

I sat down on the gazebo steps, stared at my friends and wondered, *How will we ever solve the code if this clowning around continues?*

Chapter Six

IN THE NAME OF FRIENDSHIP

"Silver Dawn is such a pretty name," I said to Grandma one day, as we were putting fresh hay in the barn stall. "How did she get it?"

"That's a good story," Grandma Goodie said. "One morning, Smooch rang my doorbell. She woke me up at 4:30 a.m.!"

"Sounds like someone else I know," I teased.

Grandma chuckled and continued. "She said that she was taking me for a drive. I told her it was too early—the sun hadn't even risen! She wouldn't take no for an answer.

"As we drove, I was lost in my own thoughts. Your grandfather had died a few months earlier, and I was very sad and lonely. I missed him so.

"Pretty soon, I noticed that we were way, way out in the country, on a bumpy dirt road. I hadn't even noticed how long we'd been driving.

"The sun was just about to rise ahead of us. It cast a golden glow on a beautiful, white and silvery gray horse standing behind a wooden fence near the road. That's when Smooch said, 'I'd like you to meet Silver.'

"I'll never forget how Silver whinnied* happily, like she'd been waiting for us to get there!" Grandma smiled at the thought.

Smooch explained to Grandma that Silver had been a racehorse until she injured her leg a few days earlier. Because of that, she couldn't race anymore and the owner no longer wanted her. But Grandma Goodie did.

"Silver nibbled the carrot that Smooch had put in my hand," Grandma said. "Silver looked right into my eyes, and in that moment we became best friends. I knew she was meant to come live in the barn and clover field behind my house.

"I added Dawn to her name because it was dawn when we met. Dawn means 'the first light before sunrise' and it can also mean 'a beginning.' I felt it was a new beginning for Silver Dawn and a new beginning for me, too.

"I rescued Silver Dawn and took care of her leg while it healed. But the truth is," Grandma said, "Silver Dawn actually rescued me. She's my hero."

"What do you mean?" I asked.

Grandma explained that Silver Dawn had helped her get through a rough time in her life.

"Meeting Silver Dawn gave me a new goal," Grandma continued. "It made me feel good to help my new horse friend. And I knew that if I could rescue her, then I could rescue other animals that weren't being well-cared for or didn't have homes."

Silver Dawn *was* a hero. I thought about that for a good, long while. Suddenly, a fantastic idea popped into my head: for the Grand Opening Celebration, guests could come dressed as their favorite *hero*.

"Brilliant!" Grandma agreed.

"Grandma," I said, "I was wondering if it would be OK if my friends came to meet Silver Dawn and the other animals."

"Any time," replied Grandma.

The triplets and the twins had been asking me if they could come to the barn and help feed the animals.

Besides that, there was another reason I wanted them to come. I was sure that once they met Grandma, they'd try harder to solve the clue so we could find her tiny top hat.

At the next meeting of The Secret Code Club, I gave up all hope that Phoebe, Parker, Peyton, Alex and Gracian would help me solve the code.

Four of them were going in all different directions, adding to their long list of "talents," which now also included Peyton balancing spinning dishes on the tip of broomsticks, Parker doing cartwheels, Gracian walking upside down on his hands and Alex jumping on a pogo stick.

Phoebe was the only one who was actually in the gazebo with me. However, her attention was completely on Betty. She was measuring Betty's legs with a measuring tape and jotting down lots of numbers on a piece of paper. All she would tell me was that she was making something special for Betty.

If only I could come up with a way to get them *all* to sit down for a few minutes and take another look at Smooch's secret message.

It clearly wasn't going to happen that day, though.

It was time for Plan B: I asked if anyone wanted to come to the barn on Sunday. Everyone jumped at the chance to see all the animals.

Although the other kids had lost their interest in the code, I hadn't. My determination to figure it out was stronger than ever.

Grandma was making invitations to the Grand Opening Celebration on her computer. I decided to make an extra special one for Grandma to send to Smooch—secret message style!

(See if you can figure it out using Julius Caesar's code shown below, then check your answer in the back of the book.)

a b c d e f g h i j k l m n o p q r s t u v w x y z
code = d e f g h i j k l m n o p q r s t u v w x y z a b c

Brx'uh lqylwhg!
Judqg Rshqlqj Fhoheudwlrq
dw
Jrrglh'v Frvwxph Vkrs!
Fdoo Jrrglh iru ghwdlov.

Chapter Seven

LOVE AT FIRST SIGHT

"The tour of the farm starts here," I told the triplets and twins when they arrived on Sunday afternoon.

First I introduced them to Silver Dawn, Romeo, Pearl, Jellybean and Toodles. It was love at first sight. (How could it not be? These animals are Adorable with a capital A.)

Alex and Gracian thought it was hilarious* when the animals followed us around like we were in a parade for the rest of the tour.

"Next stop," I told my friends, "is Goodie's Costume Shop. Right this way!"

As we entered the store, Grandma looked up from the mannequin* she was dressing in a black vampire cloak.

Grandma asked if we could help her out

by putting a Pilgrim costume on one of the other mannequins. As we did, the kids talked about what hero they were dressing up as for the Grand Opening Celebration and why they picked that hero.

"I'm dressing up as a firefighter," said Gracian. "Firefighters are heroes because they save lives."

"I'm going to be Ms. Simms, our neighbor, who is a nurse," Peyton said proudly. "She took care of my aunt in the hospital."

"I'll be dressed like Officer Benton," said Parker. "She's the police woman who comes to our school with her police dog and teaches us about safety."

"I'm making a costume that looks like an astronaut," said Alex, "because they explore outer space!"

"What about you, Alice?" asked Parker. "Who are you going to be?"

"I have my whole costume figured out," I told them. "I'm dressing up as Gigi!"

"Who's Gigi?" asked Alex.

"She's the best singer EVER!" I replied. "She's a rock star!"

"Why is she a hero?" asked Gracian.

"Because she's a great musician," I said.

"Well, Alex is a great skateboarder, but that doesn't make him a hero," Gracian said.

"Hey! Who says?" teased Alex, pretending his feelings were hurt. "No, seriously, I see what Gracian is saying. What does Gigi do that makes her a hero?"

I looked up, thinking, as if the answer would be written across the sky. "All I know is that I like her songs," I said.

But it was a good question. What makes a hero a hero?

I thought about it as we walked out the back door of the shop, where all the animals were waiting for us.

Grandma pointed to the corner where the back wall of the shop and the farm fence met. "That's where the DJ will set up his music for dancing. And all the tables and chairs will be right here so people can sit down and chitchat."

"And we're going to hang white lights to create a festive party glow," I added.

"Lots and lots of people have already sent RSVPs* that they're coming," I said excitedly, "including Smooch and some of Grandma's other circus friends. It's going to be a big, big event!"

Phoebe stroked Silver Dawn's long mane. "I wish the animals could come, too," she said.

"Oh, they're the most special party guests of all," Grandma Goodie exclaimed, as she gave Jellybean a gentle stroke across her soft, shiny fur. "They'll be enjoying the party like everyone else."

I giggled and Parker elbowed me lightly.

"What's so funny, Alice?" she asked.

"I'm thinking about Romeo, Pearl and Toodles dancing," I said. The thought made everybody smile, too.

"I can't wait for the party," said Parker.

"You know what would be fun?" I asked. "To have a costume contest."

"Oh yeah!" said Alex. "We could give awards."

"Like Most Creative Costume," Parker joined in, "and Funniest Costume."

"That's perfect!" Grandma said.

My friends shouted out a whole bunch of ideas for awards and we wrote the best ones on a list. We went back inside the shop and helped Grandma choose prizes for the winners:

a gorilla mask, elf shoes, an angel halo and a headband with bunny ears.

"Guess who I'm dressing up as for the Grand Opening Celebration," Grandma challenged me on Monday after school.

"Silver Dawn?" I guessed.

"I would if I could figure out how to make that costume." She chuckled*. "I'm dressing up as Smooch! She's been a true friend all these years—*and* she introduced me to Silver Dawn."

I imagined Smooch walking in the door of the costume shop. Her eyes would be wide when she saw Grandma wearing the polka-dotted clown outfit. They'd hug, and Smooch would feel really special being a hero.

The vision in my mind warmed my heart. But it also made me feel nervous and I quickly realized why. The Grand Opening Celebration was getting closer and closer. And I was more and more worried about solving the clue.

Grandma was dressing up as Smooch. The tiny top hat would be *the* finishing touch. The one accent that would make the costume perfect.

I'd been reading my library books on codes from cover to cover for a few weeks now. *Had I missed something that would help me solve the code?* I was completely stumped*!

Chapter Eight

CLOWNING AROUND

On Tuesday, feelings of frustration seemed to burst out of me like air from a popped balloon. I was at the costume shop and angrily pushed a box of costumes a little too hard. It bumped into another box, which crashed to the floor.

"Oops!" I cried. "I'm sorry, Grandma."

"Alice honey, is there anything you want to talk about?" Grandma asked.

"I'm a little upset with The Secret Code Club!" I complained. "They promised to help me solve the code. When we meet at the gazebo, everyone just does their own thing. It makes me angry."

Grandma put her hands lightly on my cheeks and looked me in the eyes. She told me she was sorry I was upset and that she remembered feeling the exact same way once.

"When I was the ringmaster, the clowns and the acrobats were sometimes a rowdy* bunch. I was always organizing meetings to talk about the acts and music and so on, but they simply would not sit still."

"They wouldn't listen to you?" I asked.

Grandma shook her head. "They'd be juggling, doing flips, swinging on the trapeze, jump roping eight people at a time...well, you get the picture."

I scowled*. "How rude!"

"Yes and no," she said as she shrugged. "They were doing what they loved best. I had to admit that their enthusiasm is what made the circus fun to watch. All their practicing is why it was so entertaining."

"What did you do?" I wondered.

"I stopped talking," Grandma said.

"Huh?" I stared at her in disbelief. "But you were the ringmaster."

"Yep," she replied. "I started listening instead. I asked them for their ideas. And you know what?"

"No. What?" I asked.

"Once I stopped trying to make them do what *I* wanted them to do, their talents shone through even more," she said. "After all, true friendship is bringing out the best in each other. Plus, without all those meetings, we all had more time to do what we were good at, which was running the show."

❦ ❦

During class the next day, I was daydreaming about what it might be like to see Gigi perform. In my imagination, I was standing by the stage watching my mega-superstar sing. Gigi caught my eye and waved me up to the stage where a stagehand handed me a microphone.

As my fantasy continued, we sang the chorus of her newest hit together. It was

69

amazing! I was perfectly in tune with her and—

"Alice," I heard Mr. Zapple say, "if I dropped one eraser, would I be dropping one-third of the erasers or one-half of the erasers?"

Parker knocked on her head lightly with the knuckles on her fist as she whispered to me, "Knock, knock? Is anybody *home* in there?"

I glanced away from Parker and toward Mr. Zapple. He was juggling three erasers, but he missed catching them one by one. All three landed with thuds on the floor. He sighed.

Peyton, who was sitting in the front row, scrambled out of her chair and picked up the erasers for Mr. Zapple. "I like to juggle, too," she told him.

"Thank goodness," he said. "You juggle. I'll teach. And then we'll both be doing what we're good at."

Doing what we're good at. It was the second time I'd heard that in two days.

Seeing Peyton juggle reminded me of the last time that The Secret Code Club met. The triplets and the twins were juggling, unicycling, hula-hooping, skateboarding, balancing spinning dishes, doing cartwheels, making balloon animals and jumping on pogo sticks.

With all that clowning around, I thought, *they're practically a three-ring circus!*

Oh. My. Goodness. I knew right then and there that, with all their combined talents, they really *could* do a circus performance. The Grand Opening Celebration would provide the perfect audience!

Right after the school bell rang, I proposed the circus idea to Phoebe, Peyton, Parker, Alex and Gracian. They were all for it!

"We'll all take turns doing what we're good at," I said. "Except...um...what am I good at?" I realized I didn't know how to juggle or balance spinning dishes or skateboard that well.

"Every circus needs a ringmaster, Alice," said Phoebe.

The kids nodded in agreement.

We had plenty of talent. We had a ringmaster. We had—what we all decided to call—The Razzle-Dazzle Kids Circus.

The day before the Grand Opening Celebration, there were still a few boxes of costumes to be unpacked at the shop.

It's 3:00 already, I thought sadly. *We'll never make it to see Gigi.* I didn't say anything to Grandma, though. She had probably forgotten. I knew she had a million last-minute things to do before the party the next night.

As if she read my mind, Grandma said, "Alice, let's stash the rest of these boxes in one of the dressing rooms until after the Grand Opening Celebration. We better get a move on if we want to get in the front row to see Gigi!"

Leave it to Grandma. Always full of surprises.

Just then the bells on the front door jangled. Grandma went to see who had come to the shop. I heard shrieks of happiness and ran up front to see what the buzz* was all about.

I instantly recognized Smooch from the photograph that Grandma Goodie had shown me. Her curly hair was gray now (and she wasn't wearing a clown outfit), but her dazzling smile and happy eyes were familiar.

"I'm here to pick up the Gigi fan club,"

she joked, and then added, "which I guess I'm also a member of. I love her music, too!"

Grandma locked up the costume shop and the three of us hopped into Smooch's car. Gigi's latest CD was playing, and we sang her songs as loud as we could all the way to the mall.

When Gigi came onto the stage, it was spectacular to see her perform right up close, in person. And afterwards I even got her autograph!

With all the excitement of meeting Smooch and seeing Gigi, it was hard to stay focused on my final try at solving the clue. I flipped through one of my library books and came to two pages that were stuck together.

It looked as if the last person who'd checked this book out of the library had been eating caramel candy while they were reading it.

I carefully peeled apart the sticky pages

and found instructions for the First Letter Secret Message. It was easy: the first letter of each word spells a message. I looked at the code that Smooch had written for Grandma Goodie.

Whistling icicles tiny helicopters many yo-yo fizzy lollipops owls whistling every rosy song

I quickly underlined the first letter of each word, and then wrote down all the first letters. It spelled:

Withmyflowers

With my flowers! I thought I would be thrilled when I solved the code. Instead I was terribly disappointed. Any flowers that Smooch once had must have died over 30 years ago. They were surely long gone.

And so was hope for getting the tiny top hat back for Grandma.

Chapter Nine

OOPSY-DAISY!

The countdown to the Grand Opening Celebration was on! There were exactly three hours, 25 minutes and 16 seconds to go until the guests started arriving.

My mom and Smooch were outside setting up the tables and chairs. They had strung festive white lights from the trees. It was already beginning to look like a party.

Phoebe, Peyton, Parker, Alex and Gracian came to the costume shop early. At the last minute, we'd decided to "dress up" all the animals for the party.

We rummaged* through a few boxes Grandma had given to us to make the costumes. They were filled with donated clothes that could not be sold because they were damaged in some way.

I pulled out a lovely dress that was missing a sleeve. The waistband was covered in sparkling pink sequins. "Let's use these sequins to accent Silver Dawn's purple saddle," I suggested.

"Look at this marching-band hat!" said Parker. "Its feathery pink decoration is perfect for Silver Dawn's purple bridle*."

"Here are some shimmering gemstones for her bridle, too," offered Phoebe.

"How about these ribbons for glittering reins*?" added Gracian.

When we were done making the costume, Silver Dawn looked SO pretty.

We had a blast making costumes for the other animals, too: a bow tie for Toodles the rooster, a flashing light-up collar for Jellybean the cat, a necklace of roses for Pearl the cow, and a red cowboy hat accented with a real carrot for Romeo the pig.

Phoebe told us she had something special for Betty, too. She had created an adorable

costume for Betty that looked exactly like Smooch's clown outfit (Betty's and Grandma's outfits matched!). It was made with black-and-white polka-dotted fabric and had a ruffled collar, red pompom trim and a cute cone hat.

When we dressed Betty up in it, we all clapped and got her a little too excited. She started leaping around and being a bit of a show-off in her new costume.

That's when Betty bumped into the table holding the vase filled with water-squirting plastic daisies.

The table toppled over and crashed to the floor. Fangs, face paint and clown noses went flying in every direction.

As the vase bounced on the floor, the bouquet of "trick" flowers fell out—*and so did the tiny top hat!*

Ten minutes later I gave a small package to Grandma that was wrapped in a bandana and decorated with a clown's bow tie. "You're not the only one who is full of surprises. We have one for you."

Smooch, Betty, the triplets, the twins and I all gathered around Grandma.

"What do we have here?" she asked with a puzzled look on her face. She carefully took off the bow tie and undid the knot in the bandana. Her face broke into a huge smile.

"The top hat!" she exclaimed, placing it at an angle on her head. "How did you... where did you...oh my! I am positively tickled pink*!"

So was Smooch. When we told the story, Smooch snapped her fingers once in the air. "That's right! Now I remember! I did put it in the vase! But how in the world did the clue end up in my clown shoe?"

We all agreed that was one mystery that might never be solved.

Chapter Ten

MY HERO

"Alice," Grandma called out, "do you want me to put on your favorite Gigi song so you can make a grand entrance in your costume?"

I was in the shop's dressing room putting on my clothes for the Grand Opening Celebration that was starting in about a half hour. My mom was bringing my friends back to the shop soon. They had all gone home to change.

"That's OK, Grandma," I said as I waltzed out of the dressing room and twirled in front of her. "I'm dressing up as my *number one* hero!"

Tears filled Grandma Goodie's eyes when she saw I was wearing her ringmaster outfit. "Why...Alice! You look *beautiful*! You even painted a glittery heart on your cheek just like

I used to!"

Even though I'd been planning on dressing up as Gigi all along (and I was still a tiny bit starstruck by her), I'd been thinking a lot about what being a hero means to me. It's someone I look up to. Someone who makes a "difference" in the lives of others.

※ ※

Guests started arriving right at 7:00 p.m. The costumes they wore were amazing! Some were from history, such as a pilot with big goggles, a queen wearing a long gown and a golden crown, and an explorer wearing snowshoes and a big backpack.

There were many other heroes, too, including a doctor in a white lab coat, a park ranger in a tan uniform with a wide-brimmed hat, and a scientist holding a microscope under his arm.

Once most of the people were there, Smooch made a list of the winners of the costume contest that would be announced at the end of the night. I was so proud when I saw that Silver Dawn was going to win the Most Beautiful Costume award.

The most popular guests of the evening were the animals: Silver Dawn, Betty, Pearl, Romeo, Toodles and Jellybean. They roamed around and loved being treated like celebrities.

When the DJ took a short break, Grandma Goodie spoke into a microphone. She looked funny in Smooch's costume and the big clown shoes, but I noticed the top hat was missing. I hoped that it wasn't lost again.

"Thank you all for coming!" Grandma announced. "We are so happy to share this special night with you. I also wanted to give thanks to those who've made donations to the farm. Your kindness will keep the animals here happy and healthy."

She pointed to my friends who were here

and there among the partygoers. "I hope you've met tonight's entertainment, The Razzle-Dazzle Kids Circus! The performance starts right here at 8:00 p.m.!"

To get the crowd pumped up for the circus performance, Alex and Gracian had been moving through the crowd and making balloon animals for people. Phoebe was handing out boxes of peanuts in shells, Peyton offered cotton candy and candy apples, and Parker invited guests to take home huge, round spiral lollipops.

I gave Grandma the thumbs-up and she motioned for me to come over to her. From the pocket of her costume, she pulled out a gift bag. There was a slip of paper taped on the side:

retsamgnir wen eht rof laiceps gnihtemos

The second I saw it, I recognized that it was the Backwards Cipher. Reading from right to left, it said:

something special for the new ringmaster

I smiled, knowing just what was inside the bag—the tiny top hat!

Chapter Eleven

A ROUND OF APPLAUSE

Five minutes before showtime, I knelt down to pet Jellybean and calm down a little. I was much more nervous than I thought I would be.

As I looked around I saw a wonderful sight. At least two hundred partygoers were having a grand time laughing and talking and eating. Heroes in costumes were everywhere.

There were real-life heroes, too, like one of my friend's mom and dad who were dancing. I knew that they were the volunteers who put up the fence around the farm when Grandma had rescued Silver Dawn.

I saw my teacher, Mr. Zapple, who had started a free after-school music program for kids. He was talking to my next-door neighbor,

Sammie Perez, who volunteers to drive senior citizens* to doctors' appointments if they can't do it themselves.

When the music stopped, Grandma Goodie, who was a little out of breath from dancing, took the microphone again. She announced that the circus was about to begin.

The DJ started the music back up, but this time it was a circus tune.

When everyone had taken their seats, I jogged to where the dance area had been, which was our "stage."

Out of the corner of my eye, I saw that the triplets and the twins had changed into their circus costumes. I hopped up onto my yellow-and-red podium and stood very still as a hush came over the crowd. Stretching my arms up and out to the sides, I began.

"Good evening, ladies and gentlemen and animal friends! Without further ado, may I present The Razzle-Dazzle Kids Circus!"

For the past few days, I had been organizing the order of performances, and everyone knew just what to do. They jumped into action.

My friends balanced spinning dishes on the tip of broomsticks, jumped on pogo sticks, did back flips and handstands and finally cartwheeled off to the sides of the "stage." They were fantastic!

The crowd roared and cheered.

Then the triplets came out to do a little clowning around with the water-squirting daisies that Grandma and Smooch let us borrow. The audience got a big kick out of that, and there was a ton of laughter.

For the final act, I got the audience clapping to the beat of the music. Phoebe did jump rope tricks while Peyton juggled four tangerines at a time and Parker spun six hula-hoops around her waist, arms and legs. Alex did skateboard stunts and Gracian wowed the audience by unicycling while playing the flute.

Something Grandma Goodie had said

came to mind: true friendship is bringing out the best in each other.

At the end, I thanked the audience and waved to my friends to come back one last time to take a bow with me. The audience stood and cheered and whistled.

That was supposed to be the end of the entertainment. The animals, however, decided to give a Grand Finale*!

Chapter Twelve

ABSOLUTELY DELICIOUS

Betty ran out and onto the podium, stood in her most charming pose, and then howled with glee. Not to be outdone, Toodles stood right in front of Betty. The more the crowd applauded, the more joyfully he crowed.

Romeo wanted in on the action, too. He nudged Betty, but Betty refused to give up her little platform. This got the attention of Silver Dawn, who loves the spotlight. She joined the other animals and looked at Romeo in a curious way.

Then, without Romeo even knowing it, Silver Dawn gently plucked the carrot off Romeo's cowboy hat and gobbled it up. Boy oh boy does that horse know how to smile!

I leaned in to Grandma's ear so she could

hear me above the laughing, clapping crowd. "I think Silver Dawn just created a new costume contest award."

Grandma Goodie's smile and the sparkle in her eyes told me she knew just what I was thinking.

We both joked at once: "The Most *Delicious* Costume!"

Sending secret messages is super easy and tons of fun.

In Chapters Three and Six, Alice figured out how these
codes and ciphers work—and now you can, too.
Follow these instructions and share them
with your friends so they can solve your codes.

Backwards Cipher

To use this super simple cipher, just write words in reverse
(backwards).
For example: ROMEO THE PIG as a Backwards Cipher is
GIP EHT OEMOR.

Pig Latin

Pig Latin can be written but is usually spoken (and sounds very
silly!). Here's how it works:
• If a word begins with a vowel (a, e, i, o, u), add YAY to the
end of the word. For example, ALICE becomes ALICEYAY.
• If a word begins with a consonant (all the letters in the
alphabet except a, e, i, o, u), move the consonant to the end
of the word and add AY. For example, SILVER DAWN becomes
ILVERSAY AWNDAY.

Morse Code

Invented by Samuel B. Morse, the Morse code was first used in 1837. Letters of the alphabet are written as a combination of dots and/or dashes. Put a / (a slash mark) in between the letters of words to separate them. Here's the alphabet so you can write your own Morse code messages:

A= •-	N= -•
B= -•••	O= ---
C= -•-•	P= •--•
D= -••	Q= --•-
E= •	R= •-•
F= ••-•	S= •••
G= --•	T= -
H= ••••	U= ••-
I= ••	V= •••-
J= •---	W= •--
K= -•-	X= -••-
L= •-••	Y= -•--
M= --	Z= --••

For example: TOODLES in Morse code becomes
-/---/---/-••/•-••/•/•••

The answer to Julius Caesar's Cipher in Chapter Six is:

You're invited!
Grand Opening Celebration
at
Goodie's Costume Shop!
Call Goodie for details.

Glossary

Many words have more than one meaning. Here are the definitions of words marked with this symbol * (an asterisk) as they are used in sentences.

awkward: *uncomfortable*
beamed: *smiled*
brainstorming: *thinking of clever ideas*
bridle: *a harness that fits over a horse's head, and is used to help control or guide the horse while riding*
buzz: *excitement and activity*
cause: *a reason for doing something*
celebrity: *an important person who is well-known*
chuckled: *laughed quietly*
clunky: *heavy*
crackerjack: *very good*
cracking: *solving*
driftwood: *a piece of wood that floats in the water and washes ashore*

entertained: *kept things fun and interesting*

finale, as in "Grand Finale": *the exciting, last part of a performance*

fuming: *thinking angrily*

gazebo: *a small building with a somewhat pointed roof that's open all around for a view*

ginormous: *enormous*

glanced: *looked quickly*

grooming: *brushing and cleaning the coat of a horse*

hilarious: *very funny*

idol: *a person that is admired*

mannequin: *a life-size form shaped like a body that is used to display clothes in a store*

mutual, as in "the feeling is mutual": *two people having the same feeling about one another*

panicked: *felt full of fear*

perks: *benefits*

pink, as in "tickled pink": *very pleased*

reins: *straps that attach to a horse's bridle**

retiring: *leaving a job after a certain age or*

after a certain number of years

rowdy: *noisy*

RSVP: *a reply to an invitation that you will or will not attend*

rummaged: *searched thoroughly*

scowled: *looked irritated*

senior citizens: *elderly people*

shocked: *surprised*

shrugged: *raised shoulders slightly*

shuffled: *walked by dragging feet without lifting them*

skedaddled: *hurried*

so-so: *not very good but not very bad*

stumped: *not able to figure something out*

sun, as in "everything under the sun": *many, many things*

symbol: *a sign that stands for a certain thing*

theme: *an idea for an event that creates a certain mood*

TLC: *Tender Loving Care*

whinnied: *made a gentle, high-pitched sound*

unicycle: *like a bicycle but with only one wheel*

zany: *unusual in a funny way*

this is **our** story

We are an extraordinary generation of girls.
And have we got a story to tell.

Our Generation is unlike any that has come before.
We're helping our families learn to recycle, holding
bake sales to support charities, even holding penny
drives to build homes for orphaned children in Haiti.
We're helping our little sisters learn to read and even
making sure the new kid at school has a place to sit
in the cafeteria.

All that and we still find time to play hopscotch and
hockey. To climb trees, do cartwheels all the way
down the block and laugh with our friends until milk
comes out of our noses. You know, to be kids.

Will we have a big impact on the world? We already
have. What's ahead for us? What's ahead for the
world? We have no idea. We're too busy grabbing
and holding on to the joy that is today.

Yep. This is our time. This is our story.

www.ogdolls.com

Power of a Girl Initiative

For every Our Generation doll, outfit or accessory you buy, 10¢ goes to Free The Children's Power of a Girl Initiative to help provide girls in developing countries an education—the most powerful tool in the world for escaping poverty.

Did you know that out of the millions of children who aren't in school, 70% of them are girls? In developing communities around the world, many girls can't go to school. Usually it's because there's no school available or because their responsibilities to family (farming, earning an income, walking hours each day for water) prevent it.

Free The Children has now built more than 650 schools which educate more than 55,000 children throughout the developing world. Free The Children also builds and fosters sustainable villages through healthcare, water programs and alternate income projects for moms and dads that give girls the opportunity to get the education they need.

The most incredible part is that most of Free The Children's funding comes from kids just like you, holding lemonade stands, bake sales, penny drives, walkathons and more.

Just by buying an Our Generation doll or accessory you have helped change the world, and you are powerful (beyond belief!) to help even more.

If you want to find out more, visit:
www.freethechildren.com/girls

FREE THE CHILDREN
children helping children through education

Free The Children provided the factual information pertaining to their organization.
Free The Children is a 501c3 organization.

About the Author

Susan Cappadonia Love lives in Milton, Massachusetts with her husband, Scott and daughters, Sophie and Olivia. They provided the imagination for many of the ideas in this story.

*In addition to **The Circus and the Secret Code**, she has also written eight other books in the Our Generation® Series, **Magic Under the Stars, The Most Fantabulous Pajama Party Ever, The Jukebox Babysitters, The Dress in the Window, The Sweet Shoppe Mystery, The Mystery of the Vanishing Coin, Stars in Your Eyes** and **One Smart Cookie**, as well as other children's books.*

This story came to life because of all the wonderful people who contributed their creativity and vision, including Joe Battat, Dany Battat, Alison Morin, Batia Tarrab, Natalie Cohen, Loredana Ramacieri, Karen Erlichman, Lisa Skolnick, Gillian Greenberg, Sandy Jacinto, Lisa Armstrong, Joanne Burke Casey, Pam Shrimpton, Cindy Haigh and Sophie Love.

this is **my** favorite circu

Power of a Girl Initiative

For every Our Generation doll, outfit or accessory you buy, 10¢ goes to Free The Children's Power of a Girl Initiative to help provide girls in developing countries an education—the most powerful tool in the world for escaping poverty.

Did you know that out of the millions of children who aren't in school, 70% of them are girls? In developing communities around the world, many girls can't go to school. Usually it's because there's no school available or because their responsibilities to family (farming, earning an income, walking hours each day for water) prevent it.

Free The Children has now built more than 650 schools which educate more than 55,000 children throughout the developing world. Free The Children also builds and fosters sustainable villages through healthcare, water programs and alternate income projects for moms and dads that give girls the opportunity to get the education they need.

The most incredible part is that most of Free The Children's funding comes from kids just like you, holding lemonade stands, bake sales, penny drives, walkathons and more.

Just by buying an Our Generation doll or accessory you have helped change the world, and you are powerful (beyond belief!) to help even more.

If you want to find out more, visit:
www.freethechildren.com/girls

Free The Children provided the factual information pertaining to their organization.
Free The Children is a 501c3 organization.

About the Author

Susan Cappadonia Love lives in Milton, Massachusetts with her husband, Scott and daughters, Sophie and Olivia. They provided the imagination for many of the ideas in this story.

In addition to **The Circus and the Secret Code,** *she has also written eight other books in the Our Generation® Series,* **Magic Under the Stars, The Most Fantabulous Pajama Party Ever, The Jukebox Babysitters, The Dress in the Window, The Sweet Shoppe Mystery, The Mystery of the Vanishing Coin, Stars in Your Eyes** *and* **One Smart Cookie,** *as well as other children's books.*

This story came to life because of all the wonderful people who contributed their creativity and vision, including Joe Battat, Dany Battat, Alison Morin, Batia Tarrab, Natalie Cohen, Loredana Ramacieri, Karen Erlichman, Lisa Skolnick, Gillian Greenberg, Sandy Jacinto, Lisa Armstrong, Joanne Burke Casey, Pam Shrimpton, Cindy Haigh and Sophie Love.

this is my favorite circus story: